DRAGON SLAYERS' ACADEMY™ 20

SCHOOL'S OUT...FOREVER!

For all the lads in the BOYS READ, BOYS RULE BOOK CLUB who read
every DSA book: Charlie Adams, Jack Calabrese, Jack Lindly, Joseph Nelson,
Michael Nelson, Jonathan Oppenheimer, and Jonah Werbel of
Thomas Jefferson Elementary School, Falls Church City, VA
—KM

For Kate—Thank you for creating the DRAGON SLAYERS' ACADEMY
series—it was a fun ride! And to my three grandsons: Marco and
Stefano and Thomas, who are all just learning to read
—BB

GROSSET & DUNLAP
Published by the Penguin Group
Penguin Group (USA) Inc., 375 Hudson Street, New York, New York 10014, USA
Penguin Group (Canada), 90 Eglinton Avenue East, Suite 700, Toronto,
Ontario M4P 2Y3, Canada (a division of Pearson Penguin Canada Inc.)
Penguin Books Ltd., 80 Strand, London WC2R 0RL, England
Penguin Group Ireland, 25 St. Stephen's Green, Dublin 2, Ireland
(a division of Penguin Books Ltd.)
Penguin Group (Australia), 250 Camberwell Road, Camberwell, Victoria 3124, Australia
(a division of Pearson Australia Group Pty. Ltd.)
Penguin Books India Pvt. Ltd., 11 Community Centre,
Panchsheel Park, New Delhi—110 017, India
Penguin Group (NZ), 67 Apollo Drive, Rosedale, Auckland 0632, New Zealand
(a division of Pearson New Zealand Ltd.)
Penguin Books (South Africa) (Pty.) Ltd., 24 Sturdee Avenue,
Rosebank, Johannesburg 2196, South Africa

Penguin Books Ltd., Registered Offices: 80 Strand, London WC2R 0RL, England

Cover illustration by Stephen Gilpin.

Library of Congress Control Number: 2011043284

ISBN 978-0-448-44571-7   10 9 8 7 6 5 4 3 2 1

ALWAYS LEARNING   PEARSON

SCHOOL'S OUT...FOREVER!

By Kate McMullan
Cover illustration by Stephen Gilpin
Illustrated by Bill Basso

Grosset & Dunlap
An Imprint of Penguin Group (USA) Inc.

Chapter 1

Daisy, I am worried about Worm," Wiglaf said to his pig as he sat beside her in a cozy corner of the henhouse at Dragon Slayers' Academy. "'Tis not like him to stay away for so long."

Worm was a young dragon. Wiglaf and his friend Angus had watched him hatch from his egg, and they had raised the little pipling. He was grown now, but Wiglaf still thought of him as his baby dragon.

"Orm-way ill-way ome-cay ack-bay," said Daisy in Pig Latin, which she'd spoken ever since a wizard put a spell on her.

"I hope Worm will come back," said Wiglaf. "And soon!"

A bell sounded.

"Egad!" Wiglaf jumped up. "I am late for Lady Lobelia's Table Manners class."

Daisy's eyes grew wide. *"Able-tay anners-may?"*

"Lady Lobelia serves cheese and sausages in her class!" cried Wiglaf as he zoomed out of the henhouse. "'Tis a fine change from eel!"

Wiglaf ran across the castle yard into the castle. He sped down a hallway, rounded a corner, and—WHAM!—slammed into the belly of Mordred de Marvelous, DSA's well-fed headmaster.

"OOF!" gasped Mordred. "Why, you little guttersnipe! You nearly knocked into Lady Drippingwealth and Count Moneypots!"

"Sorry, sir!" cried Wiglaf. He looked up at a tall woman in a red gown and a dark-haired man in a red tunic who stood beside the headmaster.

"Clumsy clodhopper!" muttered Count Moneypots.

"Peasant!" sneered Lady Drippingwealth.

Mordred turned to his visitors. "Come!" he said. "Let me show you where we'll put the bingo parlor."

Wiglaf pressed against the castle wall as the three swept past him.

Bingo parlor? he thought as he took off running for

Lady Lobelia's class. What was the headmaster up to now?

Wiglaf walked into the classroom to find Angus, Erica, and Janice sitting at a table. In front of them were plates—empty plates. He gasped. "Did I miss lunch?"

"Sadly, yes," said Lady Lobelia. "But you're just in time for napkin folding!"

After class, the four friends headed out to the castle yard for scrubbing.

"What good sausages!" exclaimed Angus, rubbing his belly as they went.

"Do not talk of sausages!" cried Wiglaf. His stomach growled. "Let us talk of Worm. He is still missing."

"We could go on a quest to find him," said Erica.

Janice snapped the piece of Smilin' Hal's Tree Sap Gum she was chewing and raised a thumb in approval.

Wiglaf smiled. Erica was always ready to set off on a quest. In the years they'd been at DSA, they'd gone on dozens, and Erica always led the way.

"Where shall we go?" he asked.

"I've heard of a cave where dragons gather called Fire-Breathers' Lair," said Erica. "Even if Worm isn't at the Lair, the other dragons may know his whereabouts."

For the first time all day, Wiglaf felt hopeful.

"Where is this cave?" asked Janice.

"West of the Dark Forest," said Erica.

"Uncle Mordred will never let us go," said Angus, who was the headmaster's nephew. "Who would do the scrubbing?"

"I shall ask, anyway," said Erica. "Right after class."

Wiglaf smiled. With Erica in charge, Worm was as good as found!

Now out of the castle carrying a stack of greasy plates came Frypot, the school cook. "Cut the chatter and grab a platter!" he called.

Dunking grimy rags into buckets of slimy water, the students began washing dishes.

"Uncle Mordred has some strange visitors," Angus whispered as he dunked a dish into the rinse water. "Did you see them?"

Wiglaf nodded and looked up from the plate he was scrubbing. "And—there they are now!"

Indeed, Mordred's violet eyes shone happily as he led Lady Drippingwealth and Count Moneypots toward the castle gate. He was smiling, and his gold front tooth glinted merrily in the sunlight.

"We'll throw a tent up over the castle yard and set up poker tables," Mordred told his visitors.

Wiglaf and his friends watched the group walk through the gate to the drawbridge.

"Poker tables?" said Angus. "Something weird's going on."

"That's why I love DSA!" cried Janice. "Something weird is *always* going on!"

The four scrubbed the worst of the grease off the dishes and laid them on the scrubbing block to dry.

"Class dismissed!" said Frypot. "Unless," he added, "one of you wants extra credit for scrubbing the eel cauldron."

Wiglaf eyed the cauldron. It was coated with thick, green eel slime. The smell of it made him sick to his empty stomach.

"Ooh, please! I shall do it, sir!" cried Erica, who never could resist an extra-credit assignment. This was why she always won the Future Dragon Slayer of the Month Award.

Wiglaf nudged her. "But you must ask Mordred about our quest."

"You ask," said Erica, pushing up her sleeves. "I have work to do!"

Wiglaf and Angus started up the stairs to Mordred's office.

"I'll bet you anything, he says no," said Angus.

"Will you bet your stash?" asked Wiglaf, who was still hungry from missing lunch.

Angus gasped. "My stash?" Each month his mother sent him a fine chest of goodies, which he kept hidden in a secret place. He never shared if he could help it. "Not a chance."

When the lads reached Mordred's office, they heard voices inside. Suddenly, the office door swung open.

"Farewell, Sir Fuzzydice!" Mordred clapped a white-haired man on the back. "After the graduation ceremony, we shall carry out our plans."

Ceremony? Wiglaf glanced at Angus as Sir Fuzzydice hurried off down the hallway. DSA had never had a graduation ceremony before.

Angus only shrugged.

Now Mordred spied the lads. "Egad, students!" he cried. "What do you want?"

"I must ask you, sir...," Wiglaf began.

"Spit it out!" cried Mordred, his face turning red.

"Some of us in Class II...," Wiglaf went on.

"Say it!" The headmaster's violet eyes bulged from their sockets.

"...wish to go on a quest, sir," Wiglaf finished.

"Is THAT all?" thundered Mordred. "Blazing King Ken's britches, GO!"

"Excuse me, Uncle," said Angus, "but did you say something about graduation?"

"Ah, graduation day!" Mordred's red face faded to pink. His eyes popped back into their sockets. "Yes... the sooner the better."

"Are we to have festivities this year?" Angus asked eagerly.

"None of your beeswax!" bellowed Mordred. "Go on your quest! And take every little rotter you can round up with you. Go, GO, *GO!*"

Chapter 2

The next morning, Wiglaf rolled up his thin blanket and tied a rope around it. He was packed! Then he stuck his sword, Surekill, in his belt, breakfasted on eel porridge, and stopped by the henhouse to tell Daisy about the quest.

"Ood-gay uck-lay!" said his pig.

Back in the castle yard, Wiglaf found Janice waiting beside the slightly-less-greasy eel cauldron.

"Frypot gave us food for our travels," she called, holding up a bag that smelled strongly of eel.

Erica was sitting on the scrubbing block, scowling down at a letter.

At last she looked up. "My uncle Homer and aunt Marge, who rule Palmlandia, are visiting my parents," she said. "And my horrid cousin, Rex, is with them because his parents want to send him to school here at DSA!"

"How horrid is he?" asked Wiglaf.

"On his last visit, he rode my bloodhound Rufus around the palace like a pony," said Erica. "He smashed everything in his path, including my Sir Lancelot piggy bank."

Wiglaf thought Rex sounded a lot like his brothers. Their favorite pastime was banging their heads on the table—hard!

Erica stuck the letter into her pack and pulled out a map. "'Tis a two-day hike to Fire-Breathers' Lair," she said. "Where is Angus? We must be off!"

"Ready!" called Angus, who came out of the castle carrying an enormous pack.

Just then, Wiglaf spied his younger brother Dudwin racing toward them. Dudwin was a stout, yellow-haired lad and already taller than Wiglaf.

"Wiggie!" said Dudwin when he reached him. "Where are you going?"

"On a quest to find Worm." Wiglaf sniffed. "You smell fishy, Dud."

"I went skinny-dipping in the moat." Dudwin grinned. "I want to go on your quest!"

"All right," said Wiglaf, remembering Mordred's order to take along every little rotter.

Dudwin pounded his chest with his fist and gave a loud thank-you burp.

"Yuck!" said Erica. "Give your blanket to your stinky brother, Wiggie. You can use my extra one. Now let us be off!"

In the morning light, the questers marched over the DSA drawbridge, and then they headed north on Huntsman's Path.

"'Tis still hard to believe you and Dudwin are brothers, Wiggie," Erica said, keeping her voice low. "You two look nothing alike."

"I know," he said. "All my brothers are big, beefy, yellow-haired lads. I alone am skinny and have carrot-colored hair, which my own mother says shall bring me bad luck."

On the questers marched through the Dark Forest. Every time they spied a cave, they stopped to search it, but they found no sign of Worm.

Long before midday, Angus cried, "We must stop! I need lunch!"

They all sat down on a flat rock beside the entrance to another cave.

"Wiglaf!" exclaimed Erica. "This is the very cave where we slew the vile dragon Gorzil!"

"I thought you slew Gorzil on your own, Wiggie," said Dudwin.

"Erica and I were a team," said Wiglaf.

In truth, Wiglaf had slain Gorzil by himself—but only by accident. It was his first week at DSA. Mordred had sent him and Erica out to kill the wicked dragon Gorzil, and Wiglaf happened to stumble upon Gorzil's secret weakness: bad knock-knock jokes. Wiglaf's father, Fergus, told bad knock-knocks all the time, so Wiglaf knew plenty of them. He kept telling jokes to the dragon, and the knock-knocks knocked him out—for good.

Janice pulled the eel-moatweed wraps out of the bag. "Here's lunch!"

"Pee-yew!" said Erica. "Have anything better in your pack, Angus?"

"Wha are oo alking a-out?" Angus said, his mouth jammed with goodies.

"Listen!" said Dudwin. "I hear music."

Wiglaf heard it, too. Someone was strumming a lute and singing:

*"Gorzil was a dragon, a greedy one was he.
From his jaws of terror, villagers did flee."*

Wiglaf called, "Minstrel!"

The singing stopped. Leaves rustled. And out of the brush stepped a man in green minstrel's garb. He swept off his cap and said, "For some bread and cheese, I shall tell your fortunes."

"Minstrel! Do you not remember me?" said Wiglaf. "'Tis I, Wiglaf! My friends and I are on a quest to find a lost dragon."

The minstrel stared. "Wiglaf of Pinwick! Can it be?" he exclaimed. "I did not know you, lad, for you have grown."

Wiglaf smiled. "Have I?"

"Aye, lad," said the minstrel. He turned to the other questers. "I remember you."

"We have no bread or cheese, only this." Janice

held up Frypot's bag, and the scent of rotting eel filled the air.

The minstrel backed away. "Then I shall tell your fortunes for free!"

Janice snapped her gum and held out her palm.

"You shall soon say farewell to Dragon Slayers' Academy," the minstrel said.

"Leave DSA?" Janice yanked her palm back. "Never!"

Erica stepped up and showed her palm to the minstrel.

"You," said the minstrel, "shall be known as the Popular Princess."

"I have no wish to be known as any sort of princess!" cried Erica.

"My turn!" Dudwin held out a grubby palm.

The minstrel said, "You shall fly on the back of a dragon."

"Zounds!" cried Dudwin.

The minstrel turned to Wiglaf. "I once foretold that you were born to be a hero," he said. "Has this proven true?"

"Wiglaf slew two dragons!" said Dudwin. "That makes him a hero."

The minstrel cocked his head. "Are you a hero, Wiglaf?"

Wiglaf shook his head. "I never meant to slay them," he said.

"Then your heroic deeds still lie ahead of you, lad," said the minstrel. "Show me your palm. Let me see what it tells me on this day."

Wiglaf held out his palm.

The minstrel studied it, frowning. "'Tis very hard to make it out," he muttered. "People with many crisscross lines on their palm are never who they seem to be."

"But I am exactly who I seem to be, minstrel," said Wiglaf. "And no one else."

"Perhaps." The minstrel did not sound so sure. He looked again at Wiglaf's hand. "I do see one thing," he added. "A queen shall smile at you."

"Thank you," Wiglaf managed. He liked Erica's mother, Queen Barb. She often smiled at him. Yet this seemed a most unexciting fortune.

Now Angus stepped up to the minstrel and held out his sticky palm.

"You," the minstrel said, "shall share your goodies."

"What?" cried Angus. "When?"

"Now," said the minstrel.

Angus grumbled, but he doled out some Camelot Crunch Bars, Hog Lard Lollies, and Jolly Jelly Worms.

The minstrel and the questers feasted on the goodies.

At last the minstrel licked his fingertips, picked up his lute, and said, "I must be off to the East Ratswhiskers Sing-Along."

"Before you go, minstrel," said Wiglaf, "can you tell us anything to help us find our dragon, Worm?"

The minstrel closed his eyes. After some time, he said, "A song has come to me. I know not what it means, but perhaps you shall find out."

He strummed his lute and sang:

"Soon upon a sunny day,
When families get together,
The winds shall blow and they shall bring
A sudden change of weather."

Wiglaf hoped the minstrel would soon get to the part of the song about how they might find Worm.

"The sky shall turn as black as night.
The people all shall run about.
'The sky is falling! Woe is us!
The world is ending!' they shall shout.
But one brave prince shall stand his ground,
And what was lost shall soon be found.
Yes, one brave prince shall stand his ground...
And what was loooooooooooooooooooooooooost
Shall soon be found!"

The minstrel took a bow. Then off he went, humming to himself.

The questers stared after him.

"What a crazy song!" said Dudwin.

"I don't like the 'woe is us' part!" said Angus.

"'What was lost shall soon be found,'" said Wiglaf. "Do you think he means Worm?"

"Who knows?" said Janice. "And who's the brave prince?"

Erica shook her head. "I fear the minstrel has lost his wits."

Wiglaf hoped this wasn't true. But the song was disturbing. He gathered his courage and cried, "Let us go thitherward to find Worm!"

On the questers marched.

Chapter 3

ight fell. The Dark Forest grew so dark that the questers could not see their feet beneath them on the path, so Erica lit her mini-torch and they set up camp. They choked down Frypot's eel wraps for supper, then wrapped themselves in their blankets and fell asleep.

The questers woke to a raging storm. Off they marched in the wind and rain. They plucked sourberries from prickle bushes as they went, and that was breakfast.

As they marched, the path grew steep and narrow.

"My pack is so heavy!" cried Angus. "I can climb no farther!"

Wiglaf and Erica took Angus's hands and pulled him up the hill. Dudwin and Janice pushed from behind.

Thus the questers struggled thitherward. Thorn

bushes stuck them. Winds blew them sideways. The rain came down in buckets. Yet Wiglaf felt all the misery would be worth it if they found Worm.

When at last they reached the top of the hill, the rain let up and Erica pulled out the map.

"Below us lies Killerfish River Bridge," she said. "Once we cross, 'tis but a short distance to the Lair."

Killerfish River? Wiglaf had heard of it somewhere.

"Onward to find Worm!" he shouted, and the questers followed him down the steep hill.

As they drew nearer to the swift-flowing river, Wiglaf saw that the long, rickety-looking wooden bridge over it had only a single rope on one side to hang on to.

At the riverbank, Angus set his heavy pack down on a large, red rock at the foot of the rickety bridge.

"I'll never make it!" he said.

"Watch how I do it," said Erica, stepping onto the bridge. The planks creaked, but very carefully she made it to the far side.

Dudwin cried, "Now me!"

Wiglaf could hardly stand to watch his little brother

zoom across the bridge. One false step and Dudwin would be swept away by the raging waters.

"My turn!" said Janice, and when she reached the far shore, she called, "Safe!"

"I don't want to go!" wailed Angus.

"But we must!" cried Wiglaf. "To find Worm!"

"I'm not so light as you, Wiggie," Angus said. "And this heavy pack makes me heavier still. I fear I shall break the bridge!"

Wiglaf sighed. "Give me your pack."

"What a fine idea!" Angus smiled. "But do you swear on your lucky rag not to open it and take my stash? Do you?"

"I swear." Wiglaf took the enormous pack from his friend. OOF! It weighed a ton!

Angus stepped onto the creaky bridge. Step by step, he made his way to the far side.

"Easy as pie!" he cried. "Your turn, Wiggie!"

Wiglaf swung Angus's heavy pack onto his back. He grabbed the rope rail and began making his way slowly across the bridge. He was halfway there when a gruff voice called, "STOP!"

Wiglaf stopped. He was trembling so much that the whole bridge shook.

The voice shouted: "I COMING TO EAT YOU UP!"

The bridge began to swing wildly as a pig-tailed troll hoisted herself up from under it.

Wiglaf clung to the rope for dear life. He stared at the troll.

She licked her lips with a pointy, pink tongue. "Guh-huh, guh-huh!" she cackled. "I EAT YOU NOW!"

"No!" cried Wiglaf. "You—you—live under this bridge?" he asked, hoping to change the subject.

"Yah," said the troll. "Killerfish River Bridge good place to find food." She licked her lips again.

Wiglaf's eyes flicked nervously toward the riverbank. Dudwin, Erica, and Janice were wading in the shallow waters at the river's edge and paying no attention to him. And then he saw Angus. He was gripping the rope and making his way back toward Wiglaf on the bridge. Angus! Coming to save him! Wiglaf could scarcely believe it.

Suddenly the bridge lurched again. Wiglaf lunged

for the rope as a second troll heaved himself up from underneath.

"Back off, Grock!" growled the first troll. "This lad mine! *Mmmm!*"

Now Wiglaf remembered—Killerfish River Bridge was where the troll Grock lived! For a short time, Grock had been a student at DSA. Wiglaf had tried to be his buddy, but the troll just kept playing horrible tricks on him.

"Grock!" cried Wiglaf. "Am I ever glad to see you!"

"Why, buddy?" asked Grock.

"That other troll wants to eat me," said Wiglaf. "But you can stop her, right?"

"Got any books, buddy?" asked Grock. "My sister love to gobble books."

The girl troll licked her lips again. "Mmm, Grackle love books. Books yummy. Cookbooks my favorite!"

"Alas! I have no books," said Wiglaf. "But I have something even tastier." He held out Angus's pack.

"Lower the pack, Wiggie!" shouted Angus, who had nearly reached him.

The trolls turned toward Angus's voice. Grackle's eyes lit up.

"Two lads!" she cried. "That one look real juicy."

"That pack's not his to give away!" Angus called to the trolls as he came closer.

Wiglaf's jaw dropped open. Angus hadn't been coming to rescue him. All he cared about was saving his stash!

"I have to give her your pack!" he cried. "Or she will eat *me*!"

"You don't know that for sure," said Angus. He reached his friend and grabbed back his pack.

"What in pack?" asked Grackle.

"Is goodies?" asked Grock. "From yer mommy?"

"What if it is?" Angus hugged his pack to his chest.

"I remember. You mommy send *good* goodies!" said Grock. "Marshie mallows and jiggle wormies!"

"Jiggle wormies!" exclaimed Grackle. "Give here."

"No!" cried Angus.

"We eat goodies first," said Grackle. "Have *you* for dessert." She poked Angus in the gut. "Guh-huh, guh-huh!"

"Nooo!" Angus whimpered. He squeezed his pack more tightly than ever, and suddenly an idea popped into Wiglaf's head.

"Hey, trolls," he called. "We have more goodies."

"We do?" said Angus.

"Three more packs!" said Wiglaf, flashing him a look. "Big packs! Not like this little one." He nodded toward Angus's pack.

"Right!" said Angus, catching on at last. "Three gigantic packs! Loaded with goodies!"

The trolls listened, wide-eyed.

"Carrying them slowed us down," Wiglaf went on, "so we, uh, we buried them by the red rock before we crossed your bridge."

"Want goodie packs," Grackle said, drooling a little.

"Go get goodies, buddy!" said Grock. "Bring here!"

"The packs are too heavy for us," said Wiglaf. "But you could carry them."

"Stay with lads, Grackle," ordered Grock. "I go get goodies."

"No, I get goodies!" said Grackle, and she took off running.

"You not gobble up all goodies, Grackle!" cried Grock, and he ran after his sister.

Wiglaf and Angus turned and ran pell-mell in the opposite direction to the end of the bridge.

"Run!" Wiglaf called to the other questers.

The three joined Wiglaf and Angus, running up the road and away from the trolls of Killerfish River Bridge.

Chapter 4

When the five could run no more, they collapsed in a clearing, gasping for breath.

"Nice work, Wiggie," Angus said, and he told the others how Wiglaf had tricked the trolls and saved his stash. "And our lives," he added.

"You should reward Wiggie with some stash," said Dudwin.

"Not a chance," said Angus.

"Too bad we didn't get to fight those trolls," said Erica.

"I was ready for battle!" added Janice.

"The trolls!" exclaimed Wiglaf. "By now they will have figured out that there are no buried goodies. Let us be off!"

The questers scrambled to their feet.

"Here we come, Worm!" Wiglaf cried, and they quickly marched off toward the Lair.

As he trudged up steep hills and down, Wiglaf thought about Worm. Right after he'd hatched, he was so small that Wiglaf and Angus had wrapped him in a blanket and carried him to Daisy in the henhouse. And the day Worm had first opened his eyes, he'd looked right at Wiglaf and said, *"Mmmmmommy!"*

How Wiglaf loved that dragon!

At last, signs began appearing by the side of the road.

THIS WAY TO THE LAIR!

VISIT THE LAIR—OPEN EVERY DAY!

Soon they were joined on the path by more and more people heading for the Lair. Wiglaf wondered why a dragon cave would be so popular.

The sun was high in the sky when they passed another sign:

YOU'RE ALMOST THERE!

Wiglaf broke into a run, and the other questers ran after him. But when they reached the cave, they all stopped short. Could this be the right place?

Over the mouth of the cave, a big sign said:

LAIR SHOPPING CAVE

WORLD'S LARGEST HOME IMPROVEMENT CENTER

"Erica?" said Wiglaf. "Check the map."

"Greetings!" called a hefty man coming toward them. He had black hair and a beard to match. "Alfgar, here to help you. Go on in! Carts are to your right. Whether you're fixing up your hovel, cottage, or castle, you've come to the right spot!"

"Good sir," said Erica, "we were told that dragons gather in this cave."

"They did, lass," said Alfgar. "But the dragons flew off a few weeks ago, and there was no sense in letting twenty-five thousand square feet of space go to waste, so..." He raised a hand toward the sign that said: LAIR SHOPPING CAVE.

"Where did the dragons go?" cried Wiglaf.

"Who knows?" said Alfgar.

Wiglaf groaned. They had marched through rain and mud. Sticker bushes had scratched them. They'd nearly been eaten by trolls! And here they were, no closer to finding Worm than when they had set out from DSA.

"Sir, is there no one here who knows about the dragons?" Wiglaf asked.

"One dragon stuck around," said Alfgar. "You can ask him. He runs the loading dock outside the back entrance of the cave."

"A cave doesn't have a back entrance," said Erica.

"This one does," said Alfgar. "It's so big it goes under the hill all the way through to the other side. Say, did I mention that we have a special on lumber? But if you're wanting ladders, hammers, nails, or gold paint, you're out of luck. Sent those items over to Dragon Slayers' Academy yesterday, and we're all sold out."

"To DSA?" said Angus. "But why?"

"Who knows?" said Alfgar. "But we have some nice, yellow paint. Looks gold if the light's dim."

The questers thanked Alfgar and hurried into the cave. They passed aisles of paving stones, mortar mix, gravel sacks, sod plugs, do-it-yourself thatching kits, and ready-made wishing wells. At last they reached the rear entrance and went out to the loading dock.

A sand-colored dragon was stacking bales of straw in a wagon. Other wagons were lined up along the road, waiting to get their goods.

"Excuse me, dragon?" called Wiglaf.

"Name's Bob," said the dragon.

"We are looking for a young dragon named Worm, Bob," said Wiglaf. "He's green and has yellow eyes with cherry-red centers. Was he here?"

"Yep." Bob nodded. "Said he was raised by humans. Came here to hobnob with other fire-breathers. Learn what we dragons had to teach him."

"Stop yapping and keep loading!" cried the wagon driver. "I have to make it to West Ratswhiskers by sundown!"

Bob tossed the last bale into the wagon. Then he called out, "Next!"

"Do you know where Worm is now, Bob?" asked Wiglaf.

"He was talking about maybe flying north to go to dragon school," said Bob as the next wagon pulled up to the loading dock. "Can't recall the name."

"Was it Dragon Slackers' Academy?" asked Angus.

"That's it," said Bob, loading a thatching kit into the next wagon. "Don't know if he ever got there, but that's where he was headed."

"Thank you, Bob!" said Wiglaf.

The questers jumped down from the loading dock and made their way up a winding path. When they reached a shady oak tree, they sat down to figure out what to do next. Angus took out his stash and nibbled, but never offered to share.

"Going to Dragon Slackers' Academy will be risky," said Wiglaf.

Erica pulled out her map. "And it's a long, long walk to that school."

"I have blisters on every toe already!" cried Angus. "Look if you don't believe me!"

"I have an idea," said Wiglaf. "Let us summon Zelnoc. We can ask him to put a spell on us so we can fly to Dragon Slackers' Academy."

"Remember what happened last time he tried that?" asked Erica. "That wizard turned us into dragons!"

"I never said it was a great idea," Wiglaf muttered. "But what else can we do? Perhaps he has become a better wizard by now."

"I'll summon him!" cried Dudwin. He chanted

the wizard's name backward three times: "CONLEZ! CONLEZ! CONLEZ!"

A blue light flashed, and out of the light stepped a blue-robed wizard with a pointed hat.

"Toadstools!" said the wizard. "Who summons me to the Dark Forest?"

"Me, wiz!" said Dudwin.

"*Wiz?*" cried the wizard. "Watch out or I shall turn you into a newt!"

"No!" cried Wiglaf. "My little brother meant no harm. We need your help, Your Wizardness."

Zelnoc squinted. "Ah, it's you, Woglib. You've summoned me at a very bad time. Ziz was just demonstrating the Wonder Wand. You toss it up like a baton! Twirl it behind your back! Quick! Tell me what you want, Wuglop, so I can get back to the demo."

"We raised a baby dragon," said Wiglaf. "Now he has grown into a full-size dragon and—"

"Is he too big?" asked Zelnoc. "My shrinking spell is foolproof!"

"We need a flying spell so we can fly to our dragon," said Wiglaf.

Zelnoc stroked his beard. "Just learned a new flying spell, but I haven't tried it yet," he said. "How about I turn you into puffy, white clouds that float on the wind?"

"We need to travel fast," said Wiglaf.

"Okay, the flying spell it is," said Zelnoc. "No guarantees, mind you."

The wizard began to chant:

"Fly spell! Fly spell! With my fly words,
I send these earthbound creatures skyward!
Off the ground! Up in the air!
Fly where you will, I don't care."

"I feel dizzy!" cried Dudwin.

Wiglaf felt dizzy, too. And he was growing smaller. Much smaller! Had the wizard put the shrinking spell on them by mistake?

"Fly, oh, fly, wherever you might.
Fly for a day or fly for a night!"

A buzzing sound filled Wiglaf's ears. Was another of Zelnoc's spells going wrong?

"Fly, flutter, glide, and soar!
To break the spell, say, 'Fly no more!'"

"Done!" Wiglaf heard the wizard say. "I'm gone."

Chapter 5

What's that crazy wizard done to ussss now?" squeaked Erica.

"Turned us into fliessss!" squeaked Angus.

"Woe is ussssss!" buzzed Janice.

"Wiggie, what shall we do?" squeaked Dudwin.

"Let me think," said Wiglaf. They could chant the words to break the spell. Then they would no longer be flies, but that meant a long hike to the dragon school. Wiglaf wanted to find Worm *now*!

"Let ussss fly to Dragon Sssssslackers' Academy," he squeaked. "Do you remember the way, Erica?"

"I think ssssso," said Erica.

"But I can't carry my ssssstash!" squealed Angus.

"I'm hungry for sweetsssss," said Janice. "Let'sss eat it now!"

"Oh, all right!" squeaked Angus.

Without another word, the five flies descended on Angus's stash. They ate and ate, though they hardly made a dent in the Camelot Crunch Bars, Licorice Dice, Medieval Marshmallows, Ginger Lollies, or Jolly Jelly Worms.

When they could eat no more, they spread their wings and took to the air. With Erica in the lead, off they flew to Dragon Slackers' Academy.

They flew on their tiny fly wings for what seemed like forever. At last they landed in the DSA castle yard near old Straw Guts, a scarecrow knight the dragons used for practice.

"Ready?" squeaked Wiglaf.

Together they chanted, "FLY NO MORE!"

Zounds! Wiglaf felt as if he were being stretched like a piece of toffee as he grew back into himself.

"You and your wizard," grumbled Erica, shaking out her legs.

"Well, here we are!" said Wiglaf. He felt like calling for Worm, but that would be too risky.

Dudwin looked at the castle. "That looks kind of like our school," he said. "Only ten times bigger. Dragons go here?"

"Only slacker dragons, Dud," said Wiglaf. "Slacker dragons do not like to flame villages or fight knights."

"That time Zelnoc changed us into dragons, we flew away from our DSA and landed at this school," added Angus.

"And you say it's dangerous for us to be here?" Janice asked excitedly.

"Very dangerous!" said Erica.

"The teacher dragons tried to flame us the last time we were here," put in Angus.

"Oh boy!" said Janice. "Maybe we'll see some real action!"

"Come on!" Wiglaf said more bravely than he felt. "Let us find Worm."

Keeping low, the questers made their way toward the castle. They reached it just as two dragons burst out the door, nearly flattening them.

"Oh my gosh!" cried a green-and-white-striped dragon. "Little knights!"

"Are you here to slay us?" cried a yellow-and-black dragon with a shiny, black crest.

"No, never!" cried Wiglaf. He stared at the

yellow-and-black dragon. "Taxi?" he said. He turned to the green-and-white one. "Sissy! Do you not remember me?"

"You dudes were the fake dragons!" Taxi exclaimed.

"I remember!" exclaimed Sissy. "You were under a spell or something."

Wiglaf nodded. "Now we have come looking for a real dragon, Worm. He is green and has yellow eyes with cherry-red centers. Do you know him?"

"Oh, yeah, sure!" said Sissy.

"Hooray! Hooray!" cried all the questers, forgetting that their lives were in danger.

Wiglaf grinned from ear to ear. "Where is he?"

"Dunno," said Taxi. "He took off yesterday."

"Say not so!" cried Wiglaf.

"He did," said Sissy. "I think he was homesick or something."

"Poor dude," said Taxi. "Said he had to find somebody he missed a whole lot."

Wiglaf couldn't help but think the one Worm missed was him. He wondered—could Worm be on his way back to Dragon Slayers' Academy to find him right now?

"Oh gosh," said Sissy. "Here comes Ace Lizzard."

"If he sees us, he'll throw us into the dungeon!" cried Erica.

"Or worse!" cried Angus.

"Hide behind us, guys," said Sissy. "Quick!"

The questers dived behind Sissy and Taxi, who spread out their wings as a large, pale-green dragon landed in front of them. He pushed his flying goggles up onto his head.

"Are you two cutting class again?" Ace Lizzard asked the dragons.

"Sort of," said Taxi.

"We're flunking out of Flaming class, Mr. Lizzard," said Sissy.

"All the more reason you should—" Ace Lizzard's eyes widened. "What's behind your backs? Are you slackers stealing school supplies?"

"Uh, not today, Mr. Lizzard," said Taxi.

Ace craned his long neck and peered behind the dragons.

"Flaming turrets!" he cried. "Dragon slayers!"

"Only pupils," Angus squeaked. "Not real ones."

"Except for Wiglaf," said Dudwin. "He has slain two dragons."

"Shush, Dud!" cried Wiglaf. He turned to the flying teacher. "Sir, we come in peace," he said. "We are on a quest to find Worm, a young dragon—not to slay him," he added quickly.

Ace frowned. "And what have you to do with Worm?"

"We raised him from a pipling," said Angus.

"We love Worm," added Wiglaf.

"And yet," said Ace, "I just heard that you have slain two dragons."

"Only by accident!" cried Wiglaf.

"Wiggie won't even squish a roach," put in Dudwin.

Sissy spoke up. "These guys like dragons, Mr. Lizzard."

Ace stared at Wiglaf. "Well, you don't look like much of a dragon slayer," he said.

"I am *not*, sir," said Wiglaf. "I think Worm may have

returned to our school to find...someone he missed. So we must go back, too."

"'Tis a long walk for stubby, human legs," said Ace Lizzard.

"I'll never make it," moaned Angus.

"Since you came here because you truly care for Worm," Ace said, "I'll give you a ride back to your school."

"Oh, thank you, sir!" cried Angus.

Ace pulled on his flying goggles and hunkered down in the grass. Wiglaf climbed onto his back and held out a hand for Dudwin. Soon, all five questers were aboard.

Wiglaf held on tight as the dragon ran, spread his wings, and took to the air.

"Good-bye, Sissy! Good-bye, Taxi!" the questers shouted to the dragons on the ground who grew smaller and smaller as Ace Lizzard rose higher in the air.

"Hang on for a tight curve!" called Ace as he banked to the left.

"The minstrel's prophecy is coming true, Wiggie!"

Dudwin shouted over the flapping of wings. "I'm flying on the back of a dragon!"

"Yaaaaa-hoooo!" yelled Janice, and her gum dropped out of her mouth.

Wiglaf looked down. He could see for miles. The whole flight, he kept a lookout for Worm but saw not a sign of his dear dragon. That could only mean one thing: Worm was already at Dragon Slayers' Academy!

Chapter 6

ce dropped his passengers off outside the village of Toenail.

"Wouldn't do for me to fly too near *your* DSA," he said.

"Thank you, Mr. Lizzard!" cried the questers.

Ace gave a salute, spread his wings again, and took off.

The sun was going down as the questers headed south on Huntsman's Path.

"Just think!" said Wiglaf. "Worm may be in the library with Brother Dave right now!"

"What's all that light up ahead?" said Janice.

"'Tis DSA!" exclaimed Erica. "All lit up with torches!"

As tired and hungry as they were, the questers broke into a run. They reached their school and started over the drawbridge.

"What's this?" cried Erica, and they all looked up at a new golden sign blazing over the castle gate:

MORDRED'S CASTLE OF FORTUNE

"What does *that* mean?" asked Dudwin.

"Let's find out what crazy thing is going on now!" cried Janice.

They ran through the gate to the castle yard. Dozens of small tents dotted the ground. Student teachers stood on tall ladders, and by the light of many torches, they were painting the castle gold.

"Is this some sort of camping trip?" said Dudwin.

"I fear Uncle Mordred has lost his mind!" cried Angus.

Baldrick de Bold stuck his head out of a tent and said, "Shhhhhh!!"

"But why is everyone sleeping out here?" whispered Wiglaf.

"The dorm's been turned into a bingo parlor," Baldrick said, sniveling from an awful cold.

"Bingo?" cried Janice. "I love bingo!"

"We don't get to play," said Baldrick, wiping his nose on his sleeve. "It's for the customers what's coming next week."

"What customers?" cried Angus. "What's happening around here?"

Wiglaf didn't care what was happening. "I'm going up to the library to see Worm!" he said.

"Can't," said Torblad, sticking his head out of another tent. "Lads and lasses aren't allowed in the castle till breakfast."

Wiglaf cupped his hands to his mouth and shouted in the direction of the library tower, "Worm! Worm! Are you there?"

"SHHHHH!" came a loud chorus from inside the tents.

"Find a spot and go to sleep!" cried Torblad.

While his friends spread their blankets on an empty patch of grass beside the practice dragon, Wiglaf ran to the henhouse. Perhaps his pig, Daisy, had seen Worm.

"*Iglaf-way!*" cried Daisy when she saw him. "*Id-day ou-yay ind-fay Orm-way?*"

"No," said Wiglaf. "I was hoping he was here at school."

Daisy shook her head.

"Woe is me!" cried Wiglaf. "Where can that dragon be?"

"Orm-way ill-way ow-hay up-ay," said Daisy.

Wiglaf sighed. Then he told Daisy how a minstrel told him he was not who he seemed to be, how they had nearly been eaten by trolls, and how a dragon had flown them back to DSA.

As he walked slowly back to his friends across the castle yard, Wiglaf spied two student teachers carrying what looked like a roulette wheel, and now he wanted to know: What *was* happening at DSA?

The next morning at sun up, Frypot banged his soup ladle on his frying pan: BONG! BONG! BONG!

"Up and at 'em, lads!" cried the cook. "The black bread mold is spreading faster than usual this morning, so get your breakfast, quick!"

The questers rolled up their blankets and hurried to the dining hall. Another new sign greeted them above the doorway:

WINDS OF FORTUNE DINING ROOM

"This gets weirder and weirder!" said Janice happily as she went through the line.

The questers hadn't eaten since they were flies buzzing around Angus's stash, so they ate every bite of their eel and moldy bread.

Then Wiglaf turned to Angus. "Let us try to sneak up to the library now," he whispered. "Brother Dave may have some news of Worm."

Without being noticed, the two lads left the dining hall and raced up the 427 steps of the library tower. After all their hard questing, Angus wasn't even out of breath.

"Brother Dave?" called Wiglaf as he walked into the book-filled room.

"Ah, lads!" said the little monk, coming out to meet them. "I canst telleth from thine faces that thou didst not findeth Worm."

"No," Wiglaf said sadly. "And you haven't heard from him?"

Brother Dave shook his head. "Do not giveth up hope, lads," he said. "I knowest thy Worm shalt come back to thee soon."

Angus peered out through a slit in the castle wall.

"There are crazy signs all over the place," he said. "Listen to this: *Try-Your-Luck Ball Toss, two cents. Guess How Many Jelly Worms in the Jar, two cents. Mordie Guesses Your Weight, three cents. If he's wrong, you win a brand-new penny!*" He turned toward the monk. "What is Uncle Mordred up to?"

"I knoweth not," said Brother Dave. "Yet he hast turneth yon classrooms into gaming parlors. And he hast sent all thine teachers off to Cheatin' Charlie's School of Card Dealing." The little monk shrugged. "So long as thou art here, lads, why not checketh out some books?"

Wiglaf picked *The Big Surprise* by Omar Gosh. Angus chose *The Amazing Sandwich* by Gladys Lunchtime. Then the lads went back down the 427 steps straight to Frypot, who handed them each a scrub brush. For the rest of the day, they scrubbed writing off the privy walls.

Angus scrubbed off *Mordred sleeps with a teddy bear!* and *Mordred's pajamas have a butt flap!*

"Both true," said Angus as he dipped his scrub brush into the suds.

As Wiglaf scrubbed off *Mordred smells like old beans!,* he caught sight of the headmaster hurrying down a hallway. Count Moneypots, Lady Drippingwealth, and Sir Fuzzydice were with him. Wiglaf thought he had never seen Mordred so happy.

That evening in the Winds of Fortune Dining Room, Frypot called, "All stand for the headmaster!"

Everyone popped up and Mordred swept in. His violet eyes sparkled as he made his way to the head table. Lady Drippingwealth, Count Moneypots, and Sir Fuzzydice trailed behind him and sat down.

Mordred remained standing. "Tomorrow," he bellowed, "is Graduation Day at DSA!"

"Hooray!" cheered the Class III lads and lasses. "We're outta here!"

"Not just you," said Mordred. "It's Graduation Day for one and all!"

"Uncle!" cried Angus. "What can you mean?"

"I mean you're all graduating! Every last one

of you!" Mordred smiled, and his gold front tooth glimmered in the torchlight.

Wiglaf felt sure that the headmaster meant they would graduate to the next class. That he and his friends would move up to Class III.

"I sent Yorick out to invite your families to the ceremony," Mordred went on.

"How kind of you, sir!" cried Torblad.

"Graduation tickets cost ten pennies each!" Mordred rubbed his chubby hands together. "By tomorrow, I'll be rich! And DSA will be no more."

Cries of "What?" and "Why?" and "About time!" filled the dining hall.

Wiglaf was stunned. DSA would be no more? Mordred couldn't mean it!

"Brother Dave?" called Mordred. "Where are you?"

"Hereth!" answered the little monk from a table in the back.

"I need diplomas!" thundered Mordred. "Make one for every lad and lass. Don't bother with fine penmanship. We need speed here!"

"I shalt doeth it," said Brother Dave. "But please, telleth us—why?"

"My partners"—Mordred grinned over at his three visitors—"and I are turning this money-losing dump—I mean school—into a casino. Gambling! Betting! Games of chance! That's how fortunes are made! Not by trying to educate a slew of hapless nitwits!"

"Are you talking about *us*?" cried Baldrick.

"You bet I am!" boomed Mordred. He looked around. "Lobelia? Make yourself known to me!"

"Sitting next to you, Mordie," said Lobelia.

"Ah!" said Mordred. "You're in charge of caps and gowns, sister. Don't spend any money on 'em. All right! Questions?"

Dozens of hands went up.

"No questions. Good!" Mordred smiled. "Diners dismissed!"

"But we haven't finished our supper, sir!" cried Baldrick.

"Take it with you!" cried Mordred. "Empty the room! I've got painters waiting to get in here. Out, you little blighters. Scat!"

That night, Erica built a campfire in the castle yard. Many lads and lasses sat around it.

"What do you plan to do after graduation, Wiggie?" Angus asked.

"Keep on questing until I find Worm," said Wiglaf.

"You can't," said Dudwin. "Once Father learns that school is closing, we'll have to go back home and pick cabbages."

Wiglaf sighed. "Back to my eleven brothers who punch me every chance they get."

"They won't punch you now that you're a dragon slayer, Wiggie," said Dudwin.

"Yes, they will," said Wiglaf. "They punch me because I'm not big nor beefy nor yellow-haired like they are, Dud. They do not like me."

"I'm big and beefy and yellow-haired, and I like you," Dudwin insisted.

"After graduation, I shall become a wandering knight," Erica put in. "I shall slay wicked dragons—the gigantic ones that flame villages and eat toasted villagers."

Wiglaf shuddered at the thought of such dragons.

"I shall go to the Knights' Noble Conservatory," said Janice. "I heard that they have real horses for their jousting team."

"I," said Torblad, "shall transfer to Toenail Junior High."

"Do you need good grades to go there?" asked Baldrick, wiping his nose on the hem of his tunic.

"I hope not," said Torblad.

When the talking ended, Wiglaf wrapped himself in his blanket and watched the campfire burn down. He'd been at DSA for nearly two years. In that time, a ghost had haunted the school. A fake Sir Lancelot had come for the day. And Mordred had tried to marry him off to a rich princess! Yet the school went on. Now DSA was closing. And with the high price of tickets, his parents could never afford to come and see their boys graduate.

The food at DSA was ghastly. Wiglaf hadn't learned a thing in any of his classes. But for the first time in his life, he'd had friends and adventures. He would miss that! And he would miss Worm.

Wiglaf rolled onto his back and looked up at the moon and stars. As long as he was at DSA, Worm knew where to find him. But he was leaving. After tomorrow, would he ever see his dragon again?

Chapter 7

The next morning, everyone helped ready the castle for graduation.

"I'm doing all this work," Angus complained as he and Wiglaf helped Frypot build a platform in front of the stables. "And my mum's off in Hogswallow and can't even come to graduation."

No sooner were the benches set up facing the platform than trumpets sounded and a pair of white steeds pulled a gigantic, golden carriage through the castle gate.

"My parents are *always* the first to arrive," said Erica. "Aw, flea bites!" she added. "Look who's sitting atop the carriage with the driver. My horrid cousin, Rex!"

Prince Rex wore a doublet and a pair of puffy pants. A purple velvet hat covered his blond hair.

He looked very royal, and yet something about him reminded Wiglaf of his own yellow-haired brothers.

The carriage stopped beside the practice dragon. A footman hopped down and opened the door.

"Hallo, subjects!" called Queen Barb, waving as she climbed out of the carriage. "What? Nobody kneeling? That's fine. No need to, really. Hallo!"

"I say!" exclaimed King Ken as he popped out of the carriage.

"Mumsy! Popsy!" cried Erica, running toward them with her arms spread wide.

"Poppet!" cried Queen Barb, hugging her daughter. "And look who came along with us!" she added as a slim woman stepped out of the carriage. Her hair was done up in a golden hairnet, and a small gold crown sat atop her head. She was followed by a tall man who looked like a younger King Ken.

"Aunt Marge!" cried Erica. "Uncle Hom—"

"Greetings, royals!" Mordred called, cutting Erica off. "Here are your graduation tickets! Only ten pennies each!"

"Royals never pay!" exclaimed Queen Barb.

"Never?" yelped Mordred. "Well, do you play poker? Blackjack? Roulette? By next week, we'll have it all. But first, graduation. Come! Let me sew you to a sheet." He took Queen Barb's arm. "I mean, show you to a seat."

"Be gone, man!" said the queen. "I am perfectly capable of finding my own seat."

"Yes, Your Queensiness," mumbled Mordred as he scurried off.

"Look out below!" yelled Prince Rex. He jumped from the top of the carriage, landing with a thud.

"Ow!" he cried. "My foot!" The lad hobbled around, howling.

"Rexie!" Queen Marge rushed to him.

"Fooled you!" shouted Rex, and he raced off across the castle yard.

Dudwin laughed, and Wiglaf thought that the rest of his yellow-haired brothers would have liked Rex's prank as well.

"Always joking." Queen Marge sighed. "We don't know where he gets it."

"Wiglaf and Angus!" exclaimed Queen Barb when she spied the lads. "Hallo!"

Wiglaf and Angus bowed. Queen Barb beamed a great, big smile at Wiglaf.

A queen is smiling at me, Wiglaf thought. *The minstrel's fortune has come true.* Still, he felt disappointed.

"Let me present Queen Marge and King Homer," said Queen Barb.

The lads bowed again. When Wiglaf straightened up, he found Queen Marge looking at him with a curious expression.

"Have you ever been to Palmlandia, lad?" she asked.

"Never, Your Highness," answered Wiglaf.

"Yet I feel sure I have seen you before." Queen Marge reached out and ruffled his carrot-colored hair.

"I've got news for you, poppet!" Queen Barb threw an arm around Erica as she led everyone toward the benches. "This graduation could not have come at a better time. Now you can come home and rule the kingdom."

"What?" cried Erica. "No!"

"It's your turn!" said King Ken. "We're jolly well sick of it."

"We've been sitting on those hard thrones for decades," said the queen.

"Hurts the bum," added King Ken.

"We need to get away," the queen went on. "Look." She reached into her royal pocketbook and handed Erica a flyer.

SEE THE WORLD

from the comfort of a

padded deck chair on the

Viking cruise ship *Sea Cucumber*!

Deluxe cabins still available.

"See there?" said the king, pointing. "*Padded* deck chairs."

"You're...going on a cruise?" said Erica. "But I don't know how to rule the kingdom!"

"You'll learn, poppet, and quickly, too," said the queen. "We set sail next week."

Erica looked stunned.

"You do enjoy telling others what to do," Wiglaf said to cheer her. "And the minstrel said you would be a popular princess. Remember?"

"And you're also very good at deciding things," added Angus.

"I am," agreed Erica. She seemed to be warming to the idea.

"Homer and I will stay and help you until your parents return," said Queen Marge.

"I say!" said King Ken. "When does this wedding start?"

"It's not a wedding, Popsy," said Erica. "It's Graduation Day at DSA!"

Wiglaf was happy for Erica, going home to the palace. He wished he were going anywhere but back to a hovel filled with brothers who liked to pummel him black-and-blue.

He heard a commotion. He turned and saw a crowd barreling through the castle gate. It was his parents!

And his eleven yellow-haired brothers! He was going to be black-and-blue much sooner than he'd expected.

Molwena hurried toward Wiglaf, tossing salt over her shoulder for luck as she came. As always, she wore a basket on her head for protection in case the sky should fall.

"There's our boy, Fergus!" she cried.

"Which one?" asked Fergus.

"The carrot-top," said Molwena. "You know, the odd duck. And there's our Dudwin."

The lads ran to greet their family.

Fergus greeted them with, "Knock knock!"

Wiglaf groaned. He had not missed his father's knock-knocks.

But Dudwin answered eagerly. "Who's there?"

"Howard!" boomed Fergus.

"Howard who?" said Dudwin.

"Howard you like to hear me new belch?"

And without waiting for an answer, Fergus let out a long and deafening burp.

"Wiglaf!" Molwena hugged him. "Still string-bean skinny, but you've grown a little."

Wiglaf smiled.

"And what a big, strapping lad you've become, Dudwin!" Molwena hugged him, too.

"Welcome, peasants!" cried Mordred, rushing toward Wiglaf's family. "I mean *parents*. I have your graduation tickets. Ten pennies each."

"Who are YOU?" cried one of Wiglaf's yellow-haired brothers.

"Headmaster of the school," said Mordred.

"We wants to see yer school, don't we?" yelled a second brother.

"And we ain't paying for it, neither," cried a third. The brothers swarmed toward the castle like a plague of yellow-haired locusts.

"No!" cried Mordred, chasing after them. "Nooooooo!"

At that very moment, Count Moneypots and Lady Drippingwealth came out of the castle and started down the steps.

"Saint Dominick's dog!" exclaimed Count Moneypots as the yellow-haired horde sped toward him. "What is *that*?"

"Peasants!" screamed Lady Drippingwealth as the brothers hurtled up the castle steps and through the door.

"Stop those ruffians!" Mordred shouted.

Fergus grinned. "That'll put an end to talk of pennies!"

Molwena pulled a flask of cabbage soup from her bag. Wiglaf nearly fainted from the stench. "Th—thank you, Mother," he managed.

"It's for Dudwin, silly," said Molwena. "I know you don't like my soup. The rest of the family can't get enough of it, but you, Wiglaf, have always been differ—" Molwena's eyes widened. "There's Queen *Barb*!"

Wiglaf nodded. "She is Erica's mother and—"

"Oh, I know who she is, don't I?" said Molwena. "I once spied her at the Pinwick Fair. 'Twas the year they had that two-headed calf. I snipped off a bit of her petticoat for a souvenir."

"You *what*?" cried Wiglaf.

"Wasn't I the envy of every wife in Pinwick!" Molwena smiled. "You were a newborn baby at the time, Wiggie. Say, who's that with Queen Barb?"

"Queen Marge of Palmlandia," said Wiglaf.

"Look at her, waving a royal handkerchief. Aah, she's puttin' it into her pocket and—a bit of the corner's sticking out." Molwena smiled. "Wouldn't I like to show *that* off back home!"

"Mother, no!" cried Wiglaf.

But Molwena was already making her way toward the queen.

Now Frypot stepped onto the platform in front of the castle. He picked up the megaphone and called, "Families, take your seats. Graduation is about to begin!"

Chapter 8

Wiglaf hurried into the castle where Lobelia was handing out graduation gowns.

Angus was already pulling his on over his head. "This thing's itchy!" he cried.

Erica stared at Angus. "Your gown looks like a feed sack!" she said.

"It *is* a feed sack," said Lobelia. "Dyed black. They all are. Penny-pinching Mordred. What else could I do?"

The students struggled into the itchy gowns while Lobelia gave out graduation caps she'd made of parchment.

"Stay in line!" she said, herding the students back outside. "When Mordred calls your name, go up and get your diploma."

As Wiglaf marched out to the castle yard, he

spotted his parents seated on a back bench. But where were his brothers?

The royals were sitting in the front row. Wiglaf and the other DSA students filed into the rows behind them.

How Wiglaf wished graduation were only a bad dream! He didn't want to leave his school and his friends. And when he walked away from DSA, Worm would not know where in the world he was.

"All stand for the headmaster!" called Frypot.

Mordred's red cape flapped behind him as he made his way to the platform. He smiled so broadly that his gold front tooth *and* his gold back molar sparkled in the sunlight.

"Royal persons!" boomed Mordred. "Ordinary parents! Peasants! Students! Whatever! Let's get star—"

SPLAT!

A watery blast landed inches from the headmaster.

SPLAT! SPLAT! SPLASH!

"Water balloons!" cried the students. They stomped their feet and cheered as more balloons rained down from above.

Wiglaf looked up. He spied his brothers! The yellow-haired knaves had somehow broken into Lady Lobelia's chamber and were leaning out her window, heaving water balloons!

Prince Rex leaped to his feet in the front row, shouting, "Keep 'em coming, lads! Keep 'em coming!"

Mordred ran around dodging the missiles and crying, "Stop! Stop!"

But the water-filled sheep bladders kept on coming. SPLAT! SPLAT!

Wiglaf enjoyed the barrage enormously! Yet he felt glad to be skinny and redheaded. No one would ever guess that he was kin to the beefy, yellow-haired water-balloon bombers.

When the balloons ran out, all the brothers shouted out together, "Happy graduation, Wiggie and Dudwin!"

Wiglaf slumped down on the bench. His cover was blown!

Frypot hurried onto the platform with a towel for Mordred.

"Just a little graduation fun!" said Mordred,

patting himself dry. "Brother Dave?" he called. "The diplomas!"

The little monk hurried up the steps with a big burlap sack clasped in his ink-stained fingers. He looked as if he'd been up all night.

Brother Dave handed Mordred a rolled parchment from the sack.

The headmaster called out the name on the diploma: "Knockworm!"

A Class III lad stood. He turned, smiled, and waved to his family.

"No waving!" called Mordred. "Graduation will take forever if you wave."

Knockworm walked up to the platform.

"Here!" said Mordred, handing him his diploma.

"Thank you, sir!" said Knockworm.

"No thanking!" boomed Mordred. "Takes too long. Next!"

Brother Dave held out another diploma, but the headmaster shoved the little monk aside, plunged his arm into the sack, and grabbed a fistful of diplomas.

"Liverlot! Blogwit! Chadbroth! Meechum!

Pernickel!" Mordred shouted. "Fleabane! Hockbit! Fopslippers! Up here, NOW!"

Wiglaf watched groups of lads and lasses bound up to the platform. Mordred flung diplomas at them.

"This diploma says Peawallow!" cried one student. "But I'm Leekswort!"

"Doesn't matter!" roared Mordred. "Worthless scraps of paper," he muttered. "Sort them out yourselves!"

"Angus! Torblad! Baldrick! Janice!" barked the headmaster. "Erica! Bragwort! Gwendolyn! Wiglaf!"

Wiglaf rose with the others from Class II.

"Here, here, here!" Mordred tossed diplomas every which way.

As Wiglaf unrolled his diploma, the sky began to darken.

"Fizzjelly!" Mordred called. "Coldspur! Stopgargle!"

The sky turned darker still and the wind picked up. Students held onto their graduation caps lest they blow away.

"Beltslinger!" Mordred cried.

The wind began to howl.

"It's like the minstrel's song," Angus shouted over the wind. "A sudden change of weather. Remember?"

"The sky is black as night, Wiggie!" yelled Dudwin.

"It's all coming true!" cried Janice.

Wiglaf looked up. In the sky he made out two dark clouds shaped like dragons. He stared. No, not clouds. They *were* dragons. Huge dragons! Big enough to blot out the sun! And they were heading straight for DSA!

Now everyone saw the dragons. Everyone began running around the castle yard like frightened chickens looking for places to hide.

"The world is ending!" they shrieked. "Woe is us!"

"Now Prince Rex will stand his ground!" shouted Dudwin.

"Why do you think so?" Wiglaf shouted back.

"Because the minstrel's song said so, Wiggie!" yelled Dudwin. "And Rex is the only prince around!"

But Prince Rex was running for the stables, shoving people aside and shouting, "Make way for the royals!"

Wiglaf heard his mother cry, "The sky is falling!" as she ran for shelter.

"Come on, Wiggie!" cried Dudwin. "We have to hide!"

But Wiglaf stood where he was, looking up.

The dragons winged closer to DSA.

Count Moneypots, Lady Drippingwealth, and Sir Fuzzydice raced out through the castle gate. Wiglaf heard a splash as they leaped into the moat to save themselves.

"Draw your swords, dragon slayers!" cried Mordred, running for the castle. "I order you to slay these dragons!" He zoomed up the steps and inside to safety. "Send word when you've won the battle!" he called, and he slammed the heavy, iron door behind him.

Chapter 9

veryone had run for cover.

Wiglaf stood alone in the castle yard.

Dudwin dashed out from the henhouse and ran to his brother.

"You must hide!" he cried. "These are giant dragons, Wiggie. They'll flame you!"

Wiglaf did not move.

The pair of enormous dragons landed in the castle yard, and the ground shook. One dragon was orange. The other was green.

"Hurry!" Dudwin grabbed Wiglaf's elbow and tried to drag him toward the henhouse.

But Wiglaf yanked his arm free and began running toward the dragons.

"You'll be roasted, Wiggie!" Dudwin called.

The green dragon turned its head and looked

at Wiglaf with a pair of yellow eyes with cherry-red centers.

"Worm!" Wiglaf cried as he ran. "Wooooorm!"

"Mommy!" called the green dragon, bouncing toward Wiglaf.

The last time Wiglaf had seen him, Worm was as big as a horse. Now he was as big as a house!

Wiglaf reached his dragon. He tried to throw his arms around him, but Worm's neck was too big for a hug.

"You were gone so long, and I was so worried, Worm!" cried Wiglaf.

"No worry," said Worm. *"I always come back to you, Mommy."*

"But what if you know not where I am?" said Wiglaf.

"I find you any place," said Worm. *"No matter where you are."*

"Oh, I am glad of that!" said Wiglaf. "Now tell me, where have you been?"

"Long story," said Worm as the orange dragon stepped up beside him. She blinked her deep-blue eyes.

"*This Shirley Dragon,*" said Worm. "*I meet Shirley at Lair. Shirley fly off with other dragons, and I fly off to go to school to learn dragon ways. But I miss Shirley, so I fly off to find her. Shirley miss me, too, and she fly off to find me.*" Shirley nuzzled Worm's neck. Worm purred happily. "*Lucky for us, we find each other.*"

Now Wiglaf understood that it wasn't him Worm had gone searching for. It was Shirley Dragon.

Brother Dave dashed out from the stables.

"Worm!" he cried, running over. "Thou art back!"

"*Brrr!*" trilled Worm.

"This is Shirley Dragon," Wiglaf told Brother Dave.

"*Shirley and I in love,*" said Worm. "*Want to get married!*"

"Married?" cried Wiglaf. "You are but a baby, Worm!"

"Taketh another look at thine dragon, Wiglaf," Brother Dave said.

Wiglaf swallowed. Worm was enormous. And he no longer spoke like a baby dragon. But marriage? That was a big step.

Worm bent close to Brother Dave. "*Willl you marrry us, Brrrr?*"

"I shalt!" said Brother Dave. "Where wilt thine wedding taketh place?"

"Right here," said Worm.

"Right now," added Shirley Dragon.

Mordred stuck his head out of his office window and hollered, "What's going on down there?"

"These are friendly dragons, sir!" Wiglaf called up.

Hearing this, everyone peeped out at the dragons from their hiding spots.

Count Moneypots, Lady Drippingwealth, and Sir Fuzzydice staggered back through the castle gate, soaked to the bone and stinking of eel.

Mordred's head vanished from the window, and in no time, the red-caped headmaster dashed out the castle door.

"Moneypants! Lady Drippingwet!" he cried as he ran toward them. "Sir Fuzzy!"

"Get rid of the dragons, Mordie," growled Sir Fuzzydice. "Or we're pulling out of the deal."

"Pulling out?" squealed Mordred. "No, don't even THINK it!" He turned and smiled nervously at the dragons.

"Be gone!" He wiggled his fingers at them. "Go on! Shoo!"

The dragons only stared at the headmaster.

"Fly up to the clouds!" Mordred jabbed a finger at the sky. "Back where you came from. Go!"

Worm and Shirley stayed put.

"FLY!" cried Mordred. "Spread your wings! Up, up, and away!" The headmaster ran across the castle yard, flapping his arms to demonstrate.

"I'm not doing business with this lunatic," said Lady Drippingwealth.

"Let us be gone!" cried Count Moneypots.

"Nooooo!" warbled Mordred. "Nooooooooooooooooooooooooo!"

"Get a grip, Mordie," said Sir Fuzzydice. "It's over."

Mordred's face went scarlet. His violet eyes bulged dangerously as they searched the crowd. At last, those eyes found Wiglaf.

"YOU!" roared Mordred. "This is YOUR fault!"

"M-m-me, sir?" said Wiglaf.

"Friendly dragons, my fat foot!" snarled Mordred. "They're scaring away my backers!"

Mordred grabbed the front of Wiglaf's graduation feed sack and lifted him up until Wiglaf was looking directly into his smoldering, violet eyes.

"Get...rid...of...the...dragons...NOW!" bellowed Mordred.

Angus ran out from the henhouse. "Uncle Mordred!" he cried. "Let him go!"

"Fine!" Mordred opened his fist and Wiglaf dropped to the ground, landing at the headmaster's feet.

And suddenly the headmaster's feet seemed to soar upward all on their own!

Wiglaf raised his head and saw the headmaster dangling from Worm's teeth.

Worm gave him a little shake.

"YIIIIIIIIIIIIIIIIIEEEEEE!" shrieked Mordred.

"Let him go, Worm," Wiglaf said firmly.

Worm opened his mouth.

Mordred fell to the ground with a THUNK! Angus gave him a hand up, and he staggered off after his backers.

"Dragons can be a big attraction! Think of it:

Dragon Gold Casino!" he cried as he chased after the terrified trio. "We'll make a bloody fortune!"

But Lady Drippingwealth, Count Moneypots, and Sir Fuzzydice hurried across the drawbridge with never a backward glance at the desperate headmaster.

Chapter 10

Mordred limped back to the castle yard and collapsed on the scrubbing block in a puddle of tears.

"All my dreams and schemes...," he sobbed. "Ruined!"

Now the royals came out from the stables. Other families crept out from their hiding places. Everyone stared and pointed at the dragons, but they kept their distance.

Except for Dudwin, Erica, Janice, and Daisy, who cried, "Worm!" and *"I-may Orm-way!"* as they ran to the dragons and greeted them like long-lost friends. Then they sat down together in the grass. Worm snuggled close to Shirley.

"The minstrel's song came true, Wiggie," said Dudwin.

"That's what I told him," said Angus. "There was a sudden change of weather."

"Families came, the sky darkened, and everybody ran around yelling 'Woe!'" said Dudwin.

"We thought you were lost, Worm," put in Erica.

"And now you're found!" exclaimed Janice.

"But the minstrel sang of a brave prince who would stand his ground," said Wiglaf. "But Prince Rex was the first to run away."

"*You* were brave and stood your ground, Wiggie," said Dudwin.

"But I am not a prince." Wiglaf shrugged. "Still, the minstrel did get most of it right," he said and beamed at Worm. How happy he was to have his baby dragon back!

"AttenTION!" called Frypot from the platform. "Sorry about the little interruption. Everybody sit and we'll finish graduation."

The royals took their front-row seats again. The other families sat back down behind them.

"Whoever doesn't have a diploma, come and get it," said Frypot, not bothering with names.

Some Class I lads and lasses ran up to the platform.

Frypot tossed diplomas at them and then said, "That's it! Bye-bye!"

"Wait!" bellowed Mordred, running toward the platform and wiping his tears and his runny nose Baldrick-style on his sleeve. "WAIT!"

He stomped onto the platform and grabbed the megaphone from Frypot.

"Don't rush off!" he cried. "There's been a little... change of plans. Dragon Slayers' Academy is open again. Yes, parents, you—"

Suddenly, a loud voice called out above the headmaster's: "KNOCK KNOCK!"

Wiglaf cringed. It was Fergus!

Mordred's violet eyes bulged. "Who...who's there?" he said.

"Harry!" cried Fergus.

"Harry?" cried the headmaster. "Harry who?"

"Harry up and finish your speech so we can all go home!" cried Fergus.

"Har-har!" laughed Prince Rex. "That's a good one!"

"No need to go!" cried Mordred. "School is open!"

"But, sir!" said Torblad. "We've graduated. We're done!"

"Yes! We're done!" shouted students and parents,

and they rose from their seats. There was much hugging and slapping of backs and then the families headed for the castle gate.

"Come, poppet," Queen Barb said to Erica. "Let's go home. Popsy and I have to pack!"

"Royals!" cried Mordred, running up to them. "I want to make you aware of a special DSA graduate degree. Your Erica is a perfect candidate!"

"Sorry," said Queen Barb. "Erica has other plans."

Mordred turned to Queen Marge and bowed. "Where is that fine lad of yours?" he asked. "Happy to have him in Class I! Or, is he a very gifted lad? We can skip him up to Class II, no problem!"

"We shall find a school closer to home," said Queen Marge.

"Alas!" wailed Mordred. He staggered off, weeping bitterly.

Wiglaf turned to the dragons. "Soon DSA will be no more," he said. "If you still wish to be married here, we must act fast."

He led the pair over to the sobbing headmaster. Dudwin tagged along.

"Sir?" said Wiglaf. "These dragons would like to be married here."

"Here?" Mordred stopped staggering. He blew his nose on the hem of his tunic and looked up at the dragons with damp violet eyes.

"At my castle?" he said.

Worm and Shirley nodded.

Mordred sniffed. "This castle has just had a major makeover," he told the happy couple. "Perhaps you saw that as you flew in. And golden castles don't come cheap."

"*No problem,*" said Shirley. "*My family is loaded.*"

"Loaded?" yelped Mordred. "As in tons of dragon gold?"

Shirley nodded. "*Tons and TONS.*"

Mordred bit the side of his thumb. He was near tears again. But now they were tears of joy.

Molwena, Fergus, and the brothers walked over to Wiglaf and Dudwin.

"Ready to go home, lads?" asked Molwena.

"Not yet," Wiglaf said. "The dragons are about to get married."

"We want to stay for the wedding," said Dudwin.

Molwena sighed. "I love a good wedding."

"You stay then," Fergus told her. He turned to Wiglaf. "Bring us some gold when you come home," he said. "That's why we sent you off to school in the first place."

Fergus pounded his chest with his fist, producing an earsplitting farewell burp. Then he led eleven of his sons toward the castle gate.

At the gate, the yellow-haired brothers turned and all together called, "Come home soon, Wiggie! We miss you!"

Wiglaf smiled and waved. Maybe going back home wouldn't be so bad after all.

"We miss pounding on you!" called one brother.

"And tripping you!" called another.

"And giving you noogies!" called the littlest brother.

Wiglaf stopped waving. Going home was going to be much worse than he had imagined.

Chapter 11

Everybody still here, pitch in for the dragon wedding!" shouted Mordred.

"A real dragon wedding?" exclaimed Queen Barb.

"We must stay!" said Queen Marge.

"I say!" said King Ken and King Homer together.

"Aw, blisters!" said Prince Rex. "I want to go home!"

Molwena helped Lady Lobelia cover the graduation platform with white silk. Daisy draped it with greenery that she'd gathered nearby and made a ring of flowers for Shirley's head.

Once more, the royals took their places on the front-row benches. Wiglaf thought Erica looked none too happy to be sitting next to Rex. Frypot and the few remaining students and parents sat behind them.

The DSA bell began to chime, and Brother Dave stepped onto the platform.

A large man in a black robe appeared at the castle door. A black, mushroom-shaped hat hid his face. He walked across the castle yard and up onto the platform to stand behind Brother Dave. He pushed back his hat and smiled at the wedding guests. His gold front tooth glinted in the sunlight.

Wiglaf gasped. It was Mordred! What was he doing up there? He had no time to figure it out for now. Worm bounced over and stood in front of the platform. Wiglaf and Angus hurried over to stand beside him.

Brother Dave gave a nod to Lobelia, and she began to sing "Here comes the bride!"

Shirley Dragon appeared from behind the castle where she'd been waiting. Wearing the wreath of flowers on her head, she walked between the benches to stand next to Worm.

After a few well-chosen words wishing the dragons a long and happy life together, Brother Dave said, "I now pronounceth thee dragon husband and dragon wife. Thou may kisseth!"

SMACK!

Then Worm and Shirley spread their wings and took to the air. They hovered above the wedding guests in the sky and bent their heads toward each other with their tails pointing down, touching at the tip.

"Look!" cried Queen Barb. "They've made a heart!"

"Isn't love grand?" said Queen Marge.

"Gross!" cried Rex. He stuck his finger down his throat and made loud, gagging sounds.

"Stop it, Rex!" cried Queen Marge. "I hate it when you do that!"

"Me too!" said Erica.

"Good-bye, Worm! Good-bye, Shirley!" Wiglaf called to the dragons as they flew off and disappeared into the clouds. How happy he was for them! And happy to know that Worm could always find him, even back in Pinwick.

"Awright, wedding's over!" shouted Mordred. "Student teachers? Get to work on that new sign!"

The young men picked up their ladders, paint pots, and brushes and rushed over to the castle gate.

"I'll spell the words for you," Mordred barked at his hapless crew.

"M-A-R-R-Y-I-N M-O-R-D-I-E-S W-E-D-D-I-N-G C-A-S-T-L-E. Got that?"

Now Wiglaf understood Mordred's getup for the wedding. He was planning to become Marryin' Mordie!

"And paint this!" Mordred bellowed at his workers. "D-R-A-G-O-N-S W-E-L-C-O-M-E!"

"What a fine wedding, Wiggie!" Molwena dabbed at her eyes with a lacy handkerchief.

"Mother!" cried Wiglaf. "You must give back Queen Marge's hanky!"

"Why should I?" said Molwena. "She gave it to me, didn't she? You and Dudwin tell your friends good-bye. I'll wait by the drawbridge."

"We'll park beside the moat, poppet!" Queen Barb called to Erica. "Don't be long!" The royals climbed into their enormous, golden carriage and it rolled toward the castle gate.

"How I shall miss you all," said Erica. "And dear, old DSA."

"I shall miss this school more than I can say," said Wiglaf. For what awaited him at home? Cabbage soup and eleven brutish brothers. At least Dudwin would be there with him. That was a comfort.

"E-may oo-tay," added Daisy.

"Me three," said Dudwin.

"Definitely!" said Janice with a loud snap of her gum. "After DSA, the Knights' Noble Conservatory will be so boring."

"Guess what?" said Angus. "I'm staying here." He didn't look happy. But he didn't look that unhappy, either. "Uncle Mordred said Frypot needs an assistant for baking wedding cakes, so he hired me for the job." He grinned. "Stop by anytime for a meal!"

"Be sure to come visit me at the palace, everybody!" said Erica.

Janice snapped her gum as she gazed at the practice dragon, scrubbing block, and crumbling turrets of the DSA castle. Then she cried, "Farewell, DSA!" just as the minstrel had predicted.

"Good-bye, Mordred, sir!" called Wiglaf. "Thank you for everything!"

"It's Marryin' Mordie!" the ex-headmaster shouted back. "Got that? Go on, then, all of you." He gave half a wave. "And don't come back—till you're engaged!"

Chapter 12

![W]iglaf and his friends hugged Brother Dave. Then they walked across the DSA drawbridge one last time.

Janice waved and started up Huntsman's Path toward the Knights' Noble Conservatory.

Wiglaf looked around. He saw Queen Barb sitting on a grassy hillock not far from the royal carriage. Next to her sat Queen Marge, her golden hairnet sparkling in the afternoon sun. And there, to his great surprise, was his mother, sitting on the grass and talking to the queens!

Wiglaf and the others drew near, but the queens and Molwena were deep in conversation and paid them no attention.

"I could not help but notice your fine, yellow-haired sons at the graduation," Queen Marge was saying to Molwena. "How many sons have you?"

"Thirteen." Molwena smiled. "Stocky, yellow-haired

lads, just like my Fergus. Except for Wiglaf. Who he takes after, I'm sure I don't know."

"He does seem different from his brothers," said Queen Marge. She paused. "Molwena, have you ever been to the Pinwick Fair?" she asked.

"We never miss it!" exclaimed Molwena. "Why, the year Wiggie was a babe in arms, there was a two-headed calf!"

"We saw it!" said Queen Marge. "In fact, Homer bought that two-headed calf." She turned to Queen Barb. "Do you remember what a scare we had that afternoon?"

"Do I ever!" cried Queen Barb. "Your nursemaid put baby Rex down under a shade tree and sneaked off to watch the juggler. Careless girl! Imagine, leaving a newborn all alone."

Rex stuck his head out the carriage window. "Stop talking, Mumsy!" he shouted. "I want to go home NOW!"

"In a moment, Rexie!" called Queen Marge. She turned back to Molwena. "I know this is an odd question. Perchance, did you put your baby down while at the fair?" she asked.

"That I did," said Molwena. "Oof, was he heavy. Such a big, strapping baby, Wiglaf was. Funny how he's turned out so skinny. All me other boys are sturdy as oak trees."

"Like me!" Dudwin piped up.

Molwena smiled. "I put baby Wiglaf down to nap under a shade tree, too," she went on. "I remember, for I went off to see the fire-eaters!"

Queen Marge nodded. "Your Wiglaf," she said, "has hair the color of carrots. Does anyone else in your family have hair like that?"

"Oh no," said Molwena. "Only Wiglaf is so unfortunate."

Queen Marge took off her crown and laid it in her lap. "In my family," she said, loosening her golden hairnet, "we're all carrot-tops." She pulled off the hairnet, and long, orange tresses fell down upon her shoulders.

"Zounds!" exclaimed Molwena. "'Tis no wonder you wear that hairnet!"

Wiglaf stared at Queen Marge. He had never seen another living soul with hair the color of his. What did it mean, all the talk of the Pinwick Fair and the careless nursemaid and leaving babies alone?

As Wiglaf tried to puzzle it out, the carriage door flew open and Prince Rex bolted out.

"Stop talking!" Rex shouted. "I want to go back to the palace and play my combat game!" He began running in circles around the hillock, chanting, "Wanna go home! Wanna go home! Wanna go home!"

Queen Marge rose and walked down the hill to Rex. The others followed her.

"Come here, lad," she called to Dudwin. "Stand next to Rex. We want to see who's taller."

"Me!" shouted Rex as he dashed over to Dudwin. "See? Me!"

Queen Marge eyed the lads as they stood side by side.

"They look alike, don't they?" she said.

"So they do!" exclaimed Molwena.

Rex had on puffy pants and a fancy doublet. He wore a velvet hat over his yellow hair. But in every other respect, the lads looked like two peas in a pod.

"Rexie," said Queen Marge. "I have big news for you."

Rex stuck out his tongue and blew a raspberry at the queen.

Queen Marge turned to Molwena. "Would you like to tell him?" she asked.

"Indeed I would!" said Molwena. Then she frowned. "Tell him what?"

"About the baby swap," said Queen Marge.

Molwena scratched her head. "What baby swap are you meaning, Your Queenieness?"

"The one at the Pinwick Fair," said the queen.

"I must have spent too long watching those fire-eaters and missed that," said Molwena.

"Molwena," said Queen Marge, "when you came back to the shade tree to pick up your baby—"

"Oh, I didn't come," said Molwena. "Sent me two big boys to fetch their little brother."

"Do you think," said Queen Marge, "they might have picked up the wrong baby?"

Molwena gasped. "Is that what happened?" she cried. "I always thought a bewitcher must have come along and put a curse on Wiggie as he slept, and that's why he turned out such a scrawny, little carrottop."

"That scrawny, little carrottop was my baby," said the queen.

Wiglaf's head was spinning. "You mean...," he began. "You mean..."

"She means that Rex isn't my cousin, Wiggie," said Erica. "You are!"

"I am?" said Wiglaf.

"She means you're a prince, Wiggie!" exclaimed Dudwin. Then his face fell. "But that means we're not brothers."

"A prince?" said Wiglaf. "Me?"

Suddenly Queen Marge was in front of him.

"I thought as much from the moment I saw you today," she said, and she threw her arms around him. "I am your mother, and you are my son. I named you Rex, but now you shall be Prince Wiglaf."

"Ince-pray Iglaf-way!" exclaimed Daisy.

"That pig is bewitched!" Molwena cried, reaching into her bag and tossing salt over her shoulder in case it was catching. "Come along, Wiggie," she said. "You, too, Dudwin. High time we started for home."

"Molwena!" cried Queen Marge. "Don't you see? Wiglaf is my son. Your son is Rex."

"Is he, now?" exclaimed Molwena. "Wait till I tell Fergus!" She tried to hug her long-lost son, but he ducked out from under her arms.

After that, the kings got out of the golden carriage, and there was much hugging and exclaiming of "Zounds!" and "Egad!" and "Gadzooks!" When everyone had calmed down, Dudwin spoke up.

"Will you live in the hovel with the rest of us now?" he asked Rex.

"I'm sure he'd rather go back to the palace," Molwena said quickly. "But he'll always be welcome in our hovel."

"Do those lads who tossed the water balloons live in your hovel?" Rex asked.

"They do," said Molwena.

"And what about the man who burped and told the funny knock-knock joke?" said Rex. "Does he live there, too?"

"Ah, yes," said Molwena.

"That's where I want to live!" said Rex. He turned to Queen Marge. "Don't cry," he said. "I'll visit you at the palace, and I'll bring along all my new brothers!"

"They'll be welcome," said Queen Marge. "One or two at a time."

"Where will you live, Wiggie?" asked Dudwin.

"In the hovel, Dud," said Wiglaf.

Dudwin looked glad.

"Don't be a fool, Wiggie!" said Molwena. "You never did fit in. Off with you to the palace! Fergus and I will come and visit anytime you say."

Wiglaf frowned. He would not miss most of his brothers. But he would miss Dudwin.

"I cannot go," he said. "Not without you, Dud."

"I'll come with you, Wiggie!" said Dudwin.

"Excellent!" said Queen Marge.

"What about Daisy?" said Wiglaf. "I would never leave her."

"Bring Daisy," said King Homer. "She can keep company with Moo-Moo, my two-headed cow."

"*Et's-lay o-gay!*" cried the pig.

The footman put Wiglaf's and Dudwin's packs on top of the golden carriage with the rest of the royal luggage.

"I say!" exclaimed King Ken. "Good thing we brought the extra-large carriage today."

Then Wiglaf, Dudwin, and Daisy climbed inside with Erica and the rest of the royals, and the carriage began to roll.

Dudwin and Wiglaf leaned out the window and waved to Molwena and Rex.

"Farewell, Dudwin! Farewell, Prince Wiggie!" Molwena smiled. "Won't Fergus be surprised?"

Rex burped. Then he shouted, "Knock knock!"

But the carriage picked up speed, and Wiglaf never got to hear the end of his joke.

Inside the royal carriage, Wiglaf pinched himself to see if he was dreaming. No, this was real. He was a prince! And he was going to Palmlandia.

Queen Marge sat across from him looking very happy. And it dawned on Wiglaf that this was the moment the minstrel had foretold: A queen was smiling at him.

"The minstrel was right about everything, Wiggie," said Erica. "Even about your crisscross palms saying you weren't who you seemed to be."

"And the brave prince who stood his ground when the dragons landed?" said Dudwin. "That was you, Prince Wiggie."

"It was," murmured Wiglaf, hardly believing it himself. He tried to picture himself wearing a crown. Not a big crown with diamonds and rubies like the one King Ken sometimes wore. A simple, golden crown. That would do for Prince Wiglaf.

"'Tis a long ride to the palace," said Queen Marge. "Long enough for us to tell you lads and Daisy all about Palmlandia."

"Palmlandia is an island kingdom in the south," said King Homer.

"'Tis warm there," said Erica, "with sandy beaches and palm trees."

"It—it sounds very peaceful," said Wiglaf.

Life at DSA had been full of adventure. He might miss that. And the minstrel had said that heroic deeds lay ahead of him. How could he become a hero in such a quiet spot?

"'Tis very peaceful," agreed King Homer. "Except when the sea serpents gang up on the dragons."

"Or when the giants come out of their caves to brawl." Queen Marge shuddered.

"Or when Viking pirates surround the island with their ships," King Homer said.

Wiglaf looked at Dudwin and grinned. Life in Palmlandia sounded just about perfect. He could hardly wait to get there!